Table of Contents

THE

TALKATIVE

MAN

DEEPAK GUPTA

Copyright © Deepak Gupta 2022

Prologue

There's no life that has no desolation, but there's every life that has some contentment.

'Why do you plant trees here even there's already so many greenish damn engraved alluring trees in this garden?' A man, around 35 years of age asked the old man, sigh and elevated his eyebrows & lips in dubiety, gaping for a brisk response.

The old man didn't emit a word to satisfy his mind and continued sowing mint teeny-weeny plants in a prudent manner. He had a queue of five puny plants that were demanding a soft touch of a carefully rooted plantation. The old man ignored him very well, like he was a deaf person who doesn't care for anyone's opinion.

'Hey! Hey! You, old man,' the garden man raised his voice a bit. I know you are doing a damn humanitarian work, but at least elaborate, why you are planting here.' His ill temper was about to explode anytime, demanding an expeditious response.

Winter, the stupendous legacy of god, in which everyone wants to sip a blistering hot coffee with palms, wrapped cozily in a blanket, perceiving the long dusky nights, and touching the skin of people they worship but that old man, he was purely divergent in his behaviour. When the sun was hunting for the end, he was rushing to plant more trees before the darkness could cover every inch of earth.

I know, the prolonged nights come to cuddle your loved ones for more, at least for a little more time, and small sunny days to have the opportunity to sleep more & sliding ourselves into the blanket as soon as possible; but that old man, he was super active even at the age of 52. His eyes were sharp-edged, wide open, revealing a few inky wrinkles around his eyebrows. He had a lanky body that was reaching the bygone destination and shabby clothes like that of a young man; a satisfactory contoured pant, and a classic snowy glistering jersey that was gleaming at its best. His face was almost young according to his age, revealing an immensely slight ageing, but looking a bit dog-tired with every membrane of his skin. Listening to the fierce wind and sound of ponderous flowing waves, the old man was sitting on the wild dingy damp turf, sowing some knee-high plants, parallel to the shore of the Betwa River in Orchha. Don't you know about Orchha in India? Orchha is a very bewitching dinky town near Jhansi, Madhya Pradesh. It has a flawless serene, vintage feeling and vibrant icy-cold wind where you can experience a vintage fort, abandoned peaceful sanctuary, emerald green gardens, slow-witted peace, religious eminent temples, and, exceptionally significant, a sacred expeditious Betwa River. And indeed, the town is only expanded in an area of 2KMs and situated near the banks of Betwa River. Predominantly, the town is in between the Betwa River and another end, that leads to Jhansi Road. Orchha is most popularly known as Raja Ram ki Nagri because of a Temple, named Raja Ram Temple where people worship Lord Ram as King. The town has everything; a tourist looks for like heritage, Nature, River, and abandoned places for serene and meditation.

'Not every time the God will grow plants for us,' the old man muttered a few words, coughed, and slowly shivered with the lively wind. ***Do you think, God showers rain for us?'*** The old man asked a question, promptly, raising his eyebrows.

The Garden man ignored, heated up and said, 'you talk too much actually. Plant your whatever the plants you have and the exit is there,' he pointed an edged finger towards the exit.

'Why can't you answer my question?' The old man asked again with a serious lifeless face. 'It's just a simple question!'

'Yes, I can't,' the garden man opened his eyes wide open, glaring at him for a second. 'I can't, even, I can't answer your stupid questions on this freezing winter evening. Go, live and let me live too.'

'You seem frustrated?' The old man asked with a concealed, smiling face.

'I'm not frustrated, you, stupid man. I'm just telling you to get the hell out of here, right now,' the garden man howled. 'It was my mistake to allow you to plant trees here in the Government owned Garden. Go to hell with your plants.'

The old man neglected and started sprinkling first water on the tiny plants for their nourishment. The pitch-dark night had arrived and crawled like the lustrous sacred river. His stomach had bulged inwards, looking for something, hot, pure and delicious. Just opposite to the entrance of Orchha Wildlife Sanctuary, the garden seems to be the most adoring natural place of Orchha, where you can feel the Betwa River almost parallel to the moist grass, that keeps mixing, waving and ageing in the slow flowing ripples.

After getting ears pierced by the garden man's words, the old man was still sitting on the moist grass, almost accomplished planting & staring at the garden owner who was still walking slowly, expecting to follow him just after that. When everyone in Orchha, rushing to their warm homes, the old man was quietly perceiving the nude grey sky, seeing the showering of slow-moving lights on the unlit river waves. With accumulating all his power, he stood up with the hefty watery eyes and empty stomach, crawled a few steps, and sat on the freezing bench of stone, facing towards the streamlined river. He could feel the bitter waves that were piercing the woollens of his sweater and continuously looking the other side of river, where the light was coming from, like he was on the miserable side of the river, and the gleeful part was just on the opposite, made contentment too close and still far away from him.

With impenetrable dwarf curved trees, the garden was always full of brown and leaf monkeys. It was so immense that you could keep walking through the edge of the river and reach an abandoned forest. It was quiet and a little bit scary to find yourself alone where silence was almost silent in the first place, where you could feel the paws of the fierce tiger, looking for execution. There were a few swings that were mostly empty, swinging on their own with the slow wind, frozen alone. It was like our generation keeps the most enjoyable things desolate and lonely until they die. Affirmative, sometimes the wind rushed to make those swings move and lured people to enjoy the most loving ride of the century. You know, most people, don't know much about Orchha. It's a hidden town in Jhansi, Madhya Pradesh; of course; India is really fathomless, diverse and rich to find everything in one place, that's the beauty of India; diverse culture, eternal lands, stupendous mountains, refined wind, breathe taking places and of course, winsome humans.

You know, two people talk too much, but when they get separated, they gulp every inch of silence deeply. With a small baggy bag hanging on his left shoulder, the old man brought out a stubby steel tiffin that had already frozen for a whole day. It was frosty, dense and stuffed. After applying all his remaining power, he opened the most loving dish of the children, Maggie, less and full of ecstasy but for the old man, it was damn frozen, concentrated, and had already taken the shape of the tiffin. Maggie was freezing, but his stomach was entirely empty. Without waiting, he pierced all his fingers into the cold Maggie. It was so cold that it made a strange shivering from the fingers tip to his entire body. Like we all keep our fingers away from scorching dishes, he was also struggling with his fingers that were burning from the cold. His throat got chocked with the thought of eating it, but after controlling his sense of reality, he made a small blonde ball out of Maggie and pushed forcefully into his mouth. Damn, it was frozen that made his tongue a wet piece of paper. He tried another with the intention of the last; and he succeeded too. He closed the tiffin and that was the gleeful part of his meal. The warm inside her stomach had ended and he started shivering with every wave of the wind.

'I can't stay here,' he mumbled & sighed. 'I'm seriously a stupid guy who is eating a frozen Maggie and feeling the chill wind waves of the river. Oh man, I'm really the stupid person who is talking to himself,' he laughed carelessly. 'Don't you dare to talk too much! Be silent,' he ordered himself, and stitched lips with his own burning thoughts. While shutting his own voice, he threw tiffin into his bag, and stood up with the freezing trembling legs.

'I need to go home,' he ordered himself, continued, following his own mind. As he turned to the opposite side, all the lights vanished. Everyone had gone, but he was seeing the fire, far near the exit of the garden. It was too dark and almost impossible to make the next step. He was continuously staring at the roaring fire from far away and taking slow steps in the dark long grass to reach the exit. Millions of thoughts were churning in his mind, and he wanted to shut all of them while staring at the soaring flames of the dense moist woods that were struggling to burn every moment. In a few longest minutes, he had almost reached the fire place, where the garden man saw him in a glimpse, and ignored like he wanted. The old man got the perfect hint and continued walking; but as he passed near the flames of fire, he got the best comfort of his life. He felt the light warmth and closed his drowsy eyes to make it the finest part of his life. His walk was relaxed to feel warmth for the long time, but it wasn't too long to make him feel foremost. The warmth faded away, and he knew, he had reached the exit. His legs were stopped dead, frozen as they were almost exposed to the sleepers that we usually wear in harsh summers. He looked back at the garden man and found, he was already gone. The fire was unattended and flames were reaching the heights waiting for someone to sit & experience paradise near it but after a fathomless thought, he chose the deserted road, which was the absolute truth of his life.

'I had a good life but I never cared for it,' he smiled. 'But now, I need to go,' he convinced himself, and unchained his old-fashioned hefty bicycle. The climate was frosty as hell, stealing the soul of his body. He glanced above and found some of the stars were still sparkling. Finally, with effort, he managed to sit on the bicycle and took his monotonous way to town.

As you exit the garden, the right-side road has infinity and the other has the space of town that has a narrow long bridge which can help you to experience massive Betwa River waves from both sides. It's mesmerizing and spine-chilling as hell that can make you fall into the illusion while driving on the bridge. With frigid naked legs, he kept peddling the bicycle, but very sedately & slowly, and every time a car passed, he got electrified with it. It was immensely dark, revealing only the slippery road, but the passing raving mad vehicles were giving him some rays of gleam. He was optimistic; at least he was reaching his home.

The sounds were assorted; sometimes he was listening to the wind sound; sometimes the sound of insects and monkeys' voices, sometimes a loud horn, or sometimes only the sound of harsh peddling of his cycle. The cavernous road was like life, listening and facing everything, but encouraging to keep moving, no what how slowly. The road was damp, and he was slow; but with the pace. Finally, after a few bottomless thoughts, he reached the bridge, which was dingier than he expected. The massive waves were soaring, leaving new stains on the bridge every time they fell. He gulped the empty air and moved forward with little fear. It was like a dream, where multiple scary things were happening and he didn't know what to do, but he kept peddling. The massive waves were hallucinating, luring and teasing him like a young girl lures the handsome young man. Eventually, with a few more dense thoughts, the bridge ended. He halted at the end and looked back, how hard it was actually, but he did it. He smiled, revealed a few front teeth, like euphoria was soaring in his eyes, but he was unable to express it. Ignored his contentment, he again kept peddling, went straight, passed the Orchha Fort and Raja Ram Temple, and finally took a left turn to reach his home. Even when you don't have anyone in your home, you will always try to reach home, in the hope of finding peace and happiness. Home is where we all belong at last, whether we are with people or all alone.

Chapter 1

'Today, I will plant a few more little babies,' the old man looked amused, stepping down his home's stairs like a tiger. Like every morning, he had regained all his energy once again for a sunny day. His eyes were hopeful and lips were mumbling a few words that were comforting him like a little wave of fire in the cold desert. He was smiling with his whole face that made all his face wrinkles assembled into a line. That day, he wore a pair of socks that were worn out from the bottom but hidden, making him warm, proud and respectful.

'I should choose Wildlife Sanctuary today,' the old man suggested to himself, and started cleaning his jet-black super-fast bicycle. With a calm wintery smile, he made the slowest peddle of the season. The sunshine was reaching its height along with the fog. Tyndall effect with fog was creating the dense astounding environment everywhere. That climate was the most doting quintessential weather of all time, and the old man was only looking for one thing, a tea; a hot tea, that could kiss her shattered lips with the moist kullad cup and made him feel complete and congenial. That old man was too comfortable and gleeful in the tiniest things of life. He was relishing what most people find so common for the whole life. With some hope of a tea, he checked the pocket of his pants randomly and found a wrinkled 10 Rs note, which made graceful butterflies in his stomach.

'Let's go,' he convinced himself, and behaved like a king. As the tea stall was exactly in front of the Orchha Fort, he made the bicycle move with his one hand only. In a few minutes, he reached out while encouraging and talking to the random people he was meeting on his way. That old man cherished talking too much, even if that was the beautiful and scariest part of his life. There are two sides of this world; one keeps talking and the other keeps silencing, but both are true, maybe somewhere telling something that needs to be expressed when silence should get hit by the words. Very complicated. Everyone in town knew him, not because the town was very small, but because he usually kept talking about many things to peculiar people. Some people loved him, but no one knew from where he came and what he did. Many people stared at him suspiciously, including the tea seller.

'Hey!' the old man waved his hand towards the tea seller while halting the bicycle with his legs. Literally, that, hey, was the most broken English you may ever listen to.

'Hmm,' the tea seller nodded with no interest.

'One cup of Kullad Tea,' the old man ordered, smiling ceaselessly with the confidence of money in his pocket. The tea seller was awfully uninterested, but he didn't know, every human in this world has a secret happiness that comes in the childish form, but he ignored that moment.

The tea seller poured tea into the cup which diffused the fragrance, and waves of hot tea with the fog, made the sweetest environment. The old man raised his hand towards the counter and took kullad cup with both hands. The tea was the only thing that was keeping him warm and glad. The hot waves of the cup were passing through his entire body, stretching him to get ready for the whole day. With such satisfaction, he quickly handed over the wrinkled note to him.

But before the old man took the first hot sip, the tea seller halted him and snatched the cup back, which spilled some tea on his hand, too. The warm feelings ended before the starting of the dream.

'Go and use this teared note somewhere else,' the tea seller shouted at him.

The old man's mouth got stitched, still said a few words with courage, 'But it's still a note.'

'Don't waste my time, you, old man,' the owner got furious and the old man got afraid.

'I will give you the money, some other day, please!' the old man requested in agony.

The tea seller laughed sarcastically, 'everyone says same. Go old man. Go, try this note somewhere else.'

The morning got shattered because the hot sip he wanted, fell on his hand instead. Tea can literally make anyone's day, but he was struggling to get even a sip. Somehow the sun rays looked dim for him and with no hope, he sat on the bicycle to make his way through the Betwa River bridge to the wildlife sanctuary. With no deep attention, he was peddling bicycle very slowly and absorbing the rushing sound around it. Someone was rushing with his family toward the fort, while some were making big steps towards the temple, carrying a garland of roses. On footpath, he saw an old woman who was selling clay utensils that looked so fresh, ultra-modern and charming. Looked like, everything was accumulating a heavenly positive environment except himself. In a few peddles, he passed through the Betwa river bridge, where a few children and adults were enjoying river waves on the sunny day. The waves were soaring, waiting for a slight mistake to gulp anyone's in a moment. He could feel the chill breeze that was waving the tiny hair of his hands. The bridge was so narrow that at one time, only one big vehicle could pass, but he was free of that thought. The air was fresh like it was made by the Ganga waterfall. With his deep-rooted thoughts, he blinked, boomed & he was in front of the Orchha Wildlife Sanctuary. There was a ticket window where he stared for a moment. That garden man stared at him again, but he gestured positively, like indicating and allowing him to enter the sanctuary.

The old man grinned and opened the gate on his own. The sanctuary was on the left, and the garden was on the right, and beside it, the ticket window. As he entered, an abandoned sharp feeling pierced his heart. The sanctuary was damn empty like life was getting vanished from the dying man. Accumulating some courage, he closed the gate, sat on a bicycle, and started peddling. That silence was much noisy; the birds were wandering and chirping like he entered their kingdom. The sun rays were peeping through the dark leaves, leaving a sense of warmth on the soil. Leaves were crackling, like they fell a few minutes ago and dried after. Everything was fresh, still gloomy and dark. The way was almost rough, narrow, rocky, and untouched; & every time he reached the end, a few branches of new way, and then more branches, like a new plant is growing very fast, leaving the evidence of branches. With every lost moment, he picked any random way and got lost on it. He wanted to be lost and leaving situations on their own but still cycling on the path in some hope. After a few minutes, he saw the sky who was playing hide and seek and felt damn tired, like he regained soul in his body again. As soon as he ceased, he saw a watchtower, Ekant Watchtower, whose height was really admirable, from which you could see the entire forest much farther in a few seconds. He got eccentric and left the bicycle with no care. Taking slow steps, he started to step up the stairs with a glow in his eyes. The sturdy cemented stairs were silent, but he was afraid of a wild animal that could kill him in a second. A little fear was resembling, but he was alive, at least. After stepping a few damn cold stairs, he reached the top of the tower but before he could see anything, his eyes got astonished to see a fresh young man, who was sitting there quietly with the closed eyes. It was a moment that really needed a moment to think, what the man was doing all alone on the top of a tower. Without making any audible noise, he took his way into one corner of the cemented seat. It was an L-shaped cemented seat where they both took the corners. The wind was firm, and the old man looked around to acmire the beauty of nature. The sun was still shining at its best, struggling with the white clouds, and the strange man hadn't still noticed the old man. In a few minutes, the strange man opened his eyes slowly to regain the light of his surroundings, but before everything, his new fear got unlocked. As he saw the old man, his soul got thrashed like someone was stealing his soul very harshly. It was like, he was in deep meditation, asked for a wish, and the man was there.

The strange man didn't utter a work, maybe regaining the moment of what actually had happened. The old man wanted to talk, but he was still silent and confused for no reason.

'Hello!' the strange man said his first words, hesitated, cleared his throat to say more unplanned words.

'Hello,' replied the old man, with a hesitating smile. 'Ah! What were you doing?' He hesitated and added more words in expectation of some answer.

'Actually, I was doing meditation,' he replied, blinking eyes to depict his interest in the conversation.

'Here?' the old man got astonished.

'Yes here!' The strange man laughed like a flower bloom. 'Am I doing something wrong?'

'No, no! I was just asking. You are the first person I have ever found doing mediation here on the tower in between the woods.'

'You will not believe,' the strange man got excited. 'I came here in Orchha to do mediation only. You know the situation of peace these days. Everything is rushing. This abandoned sanctuary is best to get serene environment for my meditation. Oh, I'm sorry. I haven't asked your name yet!' The strange man said with a deep infectious smile.

'My name?' The old man's lips got tightened. It was a rare moment when someone asked his name because he was much popular as the talkative man who keeps talking to people for no special reason. Sometimes people find him very irritating and puzzling to say anything to anybody.

'Yes, your name!' He asked again with whole blank smiling face. 'Okay, you haven't asked my name yet. I'm Rishi. Now, your good name?'

'Your name is nice,' the old man smiled. 'My name is Ve...Vedant,' he stammered for the first time. A few drops of sweat on his face were resembling his nervousness and tiredness.

Rishi was a young man like a new novel that needs to be read deeply, page by page, and eagerly opened by someone to be finished soon. He had a goblet-shaped face with the immense glow of a young man with a thin sharp beard and was wearing a pitch-black track suit.

'Are you all right?' Rishi asked and offered him a water bottle. 'Drink some water.'

Rishi was behaving very kindly, and it was the first time, Vedant, the old man was silent for someone's kindness that he was trying to absorb. As the old man was really thirsty, he grabbed the bottle in a moment and drank a couple of full throats of cold water. As water reached his warm stomach, he regained his sense again.

"Thank you, young man for water,' Vedant beamed, handed over the water bottle to him.

'Oh, it's okay, it's okay,' Rishi nodded positively. 'So....you are?' he hesitated to ask. 'Are you a traveller?' He asked in a hurry.

Vedant laughed like he had already become comfortable with him. 'No, no I'm not a traveller. I have been living here for many years, and you, sir?'

'Oh, I'm a traveller, mostly in search of peace,' Rishi smiled. 'I think you are the first person I'm talking well & much in this town.

Of course, it's really awkward when two persons in the same environment are silent, but people don't feel awkward when the whole world just moves in a deep dark silence. This world is weird, doing what they find really true.

'Haha!' the old man laughed. 'I think you were the only person I didn't talk in this small town.'

They both laughed in unison, and the pure laughs were echoing into the empty woods. It was like they already knew each other before, and damn now they are locked in a deep fist of a moment.

'So, you do mediation here?' The old man raised the same question again to initiate more talking.

'Yeah, I do it every day! I'm residing in Betwa Retreat Hotel. You know the hotel, which is near Betwa River?'

'Yes sir, I know and as far I know, they have the unique comfortable white tents, Vedant explained in confidence.

'Yes, haha, by the way, I also love to do camping, in between the woods and sometimes on plains or mountains,' Rishi smiled sarcastically.

'So, you are wandering here for some reason?' the strange man asked.

'No, not a special reason, just exploring, nothing. Many old men wander in search of nothing. Sometimes nothing is much important when you are old and tired.'

'You talk psychologically, my man,' Rishi got impressed. 'Okay, that's great, you can continue your exploration. I also need to do a mediation for 30 minutes more. It's really nice to talk to you.'

'You too, sir,' the old man gestured.

Vedant's stomach was entirely empty, and as soon as he checked his bag randomly, he found a perfect round thing, and he remembered, he had a guava. He stood up in excitement. As soon as Vedant said, Rishi restored his meditation space and the strange man went down the steep stairs and took his way ahead to the deep river. Yes, there was also a God Hanuman ancient temple and river inside, almost at the end. With big hopes & little things, Vedant planned tc eat guava under warm sunrays, near the river. He sat on his bicycle quickly and peddled it toward the river. The scorching sun was at its peak, waiting to become dull soon because the winter was continuously fighting with it. With some quick paddles, he reached the shore of the river, which was entirely surrounded by giant rocks, like they were protecting the soil rough planes from the high waves. As soon as he saw the gorgeous swift-flowing river, he left his bicycle carelessly, knowing there was no one except him. Excitedly, he was jumping from one stone to another, keeping his balance good, and finally, reached the last stone that was almost dipped in the shore of the river.

While balancing his own body, he sat on the cold stone & put his cold feet into the slight warm waves. It was a nice tranquil therapy listening to the slow waves and keeping legs in it. The sun rays on the waves were adding a big cherry on the cake. Forgetting everything in a moment, he cut the guava and started to eat it piece by piece. Now, he had no thought in his mind except about the strange man he had met a few minutes ago. A small respectful attentive gesture by Rishi made his day. While biting, he was seeing the shady woods that were on the other side of the river, looking creepy as hell, but in a moment, he ignored and then focused on the harsh sun rays. He was consciously teaching himself to focus on the good things. He had nothing but still focusing on the things that make life winsome. After last bite, Vedant's thoughts got ended and he felt very energetic after the therapy; the therapy that was given by nature, absolutely free of cost. Soon after, he also, realised his legs were frozen too. He smiled and forgot the thought in a second. Now he was ready to go home, but as he stood and moved back, he saw Rishi, the meditation man he had met a few minutes ago.

'Hey man,' Rishi smiled and waved his hand happily. 'What are you doing here? I didn't know we would meet again and even on the same day.'

Vedant's body got filled with happiness like he was waiting for him, silently, yelling his name from his heart, and now he was here.

'I was just....I was just eating guava here,' Vedant stammered & scratched his head full of grey hair, still balancing on the last rock beside the flowing water. The sun was chasing him from behind.

'Oh, that's good!' Rishi was surprised. 'Don't you give me some? Would you?'

'Actually,' Vedant got embarrassed. 'I had only one and I have eaten it already.'

It was the first time someone asked for something from him and he had nothing to give. He felt sad.

'Hey, it's okay!' Rishi calmed his heart.

'Okay, okay,' Vedant nodded and took his step toward the second stone.

'Oh, wait there,' Rishi halted him. 'I'm coming. Let me show what you were doing.'

Vedant got surprised, even though he was a talkative man, and now he had a person who was ready to talk and listen to him. So, what was the problem. Sometimes more kindness is seen as baffling in our society. People don't appreciate kindness; see it as perplexing, but Rishi was actually pure with his words and actions. It was indigestible to absorb such pure kindness.

'Yeah.... ye.....yeah,' the old man stammered again in fear, thinking fast about his unknowingly strange thoughts.

Rishi took some big young steps on stones and reached the last one in a few seconds, but before he could get the glimpse of the old man, the mesmerizing view of the river took his breathe away.

'Oh my god! Oh my god!' A few golden words came out of his mouth.

Vedant got surprised and asked, 'are you seeing this river for the first time?'

'Yes of course,' Rishi said, grabbed his hand, lightly, made him sit and he also sat beside the old man. 'This is magical, man! You are extremely lucky to live here. We, city people take holidays to see such breathe taking view.'

The old man smirked and said nothing.

'Do you want something to eat?' Rishi asked while checking his bag.

Vedant was still hungry, but what could he do, directly, ask a young man for something to eat? He felt a little embarrassed and said, 'no, no, it's okay, sir.'

'I have two apples, take it my friend,' Rishi insisted, took his hand and put an apple on his palm.

'No, no sir, it's okay,' now the old man felt more embarrassed.

'First of all, I'm not your sir. You are older than me; why are you calling me, sir?'

'I don't know. I just feel you are more respectable,' the old man uttered some golden words.

'Rishi, that's my name,' he laughed. 'Don't you dare to call me sir. I will take my apple back.'

Vedant smiled and felt like heaven on the stone. A little care was healing his heart rapidly.

While absorbing a lot of positive vibes, Rishi took a first bite of apple and by seeing the same, Vedant copied. Everything was silent, but the old man wanted to talk. He wanted to express his emotions but didn't accumulate the courage to speak. Again, he took the second bite and the old man followed, but before Rishi could bite the third, a monkey came out of somewhere and snatched his half-eaten apple.

'Oh shit,' Rishi got surprised. He was so comfortable that he didn't even make an effort to take it back.

'One thing you should know about this sanctuary,' the old man suggested, trying to make a conversation. 'There are lot of monkeys here even a lot of wild animals that are in the deep woods. I have seen wild pigs that could smell you from far and run behind you, of course that may take your soul away in a second.'

'Really,' Rishi's face got pale and dark.

'That's why it's a sanctuary,' Vedant smiled. 'You don't know what's coming for you in the name of adventure. Even this river has crocodiles and snakes too.'

As soon as Rishi listened, he took his legs out. 'Are you pulling my legs?' Rishi asked sarcastically.

'No, I'm saying the truth. But these creatures lie in still water, not in flowing water. I'm not pulling your leg, but if it was still water, someone else may have.'

'How do you have such vast experience?' Rishi surprised.

'It's the only thing I know,' Vedant hesitated. 'I'm just repeating the same thing I usually tell other people.

'Oh, that's impressive,' Rishi smiled again. 'Hey, I heard you about saying, you are a talkative man?'

'Yeah, I'm. I love to talk. I love to express myself, but most people don't listen to the old man who has already failed in his life. So, I just utter and people ignore me like they always do. I think you are the rare one who is listening to my shitty talk. Who wants to talk to strangers these days? People even abandon their loved ones, so what kind of important person I'm for anyone.'

The river was flowing at its maximum and the sun was going to its minimum. The winter was capturing the woods, telling them to go as soon as possible. Birds were wandering rapidly, reaching their nests, and two people were alone in the woods, talking about the things most humans ignore.

'You are so talkative, man,' Rishi said sarcastically. 'But somewhere you say things that are right. People don't listen to you because you say something they can't understand. Maybe they don't feel any connection with your words.'

'I don't know,' the old man nodded negatively. 'I think we need to go. We have to cover a long way. Are you getting out with me?'

'Of course, what do you think? Am I going to live here?' Rishi laughed out loud.

The sun had almost set and only the teal sky had left, depicting a little chance to exit the sanctuary before it turned into a horrendous wood. Their bodies were shivering somewhere, and rapidly, they took the big steps on stones and reached the moist soil to take their long way

'How did you come here?' The old man asked.

'On my long foot, sir!' Rishi blinked. 'Can you give me a ride on your bicycle if you don't mind?' He requested calmly.

'I have no problem but...' Vedant hesitated, tired.

'Oh, I will ride the bicycle, is that okay?' He asked in hope.

'Yeah, Okay!' The old man nodded positively, and they sat on the bicycle; the old man in the back, and the young man in command. As soon as they sat, the young man started paddling with all his leftover energy. It was extremely tough because the raw soil was moist and the way was extremely narrow. Sometimes they were going up, sometimes down, making everything a big risky mess, but they continued.

'So, you are Vedant, right?' Rishi asked while taking heavy breaths, peddling swiftly.

'Yes sir,' the old man answered very loudly, trying to dominate on the paddling noise, gripping bicycle very tightly

'You are a nice person,' Rishi smiled, heavy breaths continuing.

'Thank you, sir! But I think you are too nice. I didn't do anything that made me nice.'

'Even if you don't feel, keep it man,' Rishi insisted loudly. 'We all are bad in someone's story. What's so strange about it. So, what makes your name special?' Rishi asked, continuing, peddling, but slowly, reaching half way to the exit.

'I don't know! when I was born, I had this name,' the old man answered honestly.

'Haha!' Rishi guffawed as that echoed into the woods. 'You are honest. I didn't have anything to ask for, so I asked something randomly. You are a talkative man, come on you can initiate a conversation.'

'Yeah, you are saying it right,' the old man smiled in pain, like something had pierced his heart a few seconds ago. Sometimes the talkative man feels the most pain when they are silent. People love talking so, they don't get time to think about their own pain.

'Are you suffering from some pain?' Rishi halted the bicycle in between and looked directly into his eye. The old man's face was silent like a dark night with some shooting stars.

'Hey man,' Rishi's voice & eyes got serious. 'I don't know what you are suffering from but it's okay. Everyone is in some pain. Pain is a part of life. If you want to share something with me, you can. At least, I can listen.'

'I think, no one can solve it,' the old man halted the flow of tears controllably and then wiped in a moment. 'You have already done a lot to this poor old man and I don't have anything to give it to you.'

'Why do you always think, you don't have anything to give!' Rishi gestured positively. 'You have the most beautiful words & emotions. Sometimes love needs to be expressed when silence fails. Not every time people understand love in silence; love needs to be expressed deeply, that's very few people actually know. You know, people just walk away in a blink.'

'You are right,' Vedant smiled forcefully, ignored, and absorbed his words at the same time. 'I think we need to go forward. I hope you don't want to get hunted by wild pigs.'

'Haha, yes sir,' Rishi laughed and started paddling again, even faster than before. In a few minutes, they reached the exit that revealed some of the bright lights, changing their mood to happiness state. In the dark, they talked about the brightest things of their lives. It was a rare time when both were talking and understanding at the same time. That talk was damn deeper than a big ocean.

As they reached, they both stood near the entrance of the garden. There was a velvet coloured car, stealing everyone's attention.

'Okay, now I will drop you at your home,' Rishi ordered.

'No, no, it's okay. I have some work in the garden,' the old man hesitated as usual. 'I have to bed out a pair of tiny plants in the garden.'

'What?' Rishi chuckled so loudly that it took him a few seconds to control. 'You work here?' he got serious in the gesture of respect.

'No, I don't work here. I just keep planting every day.'

'But there are already a lot of huge trees & plants in this garden. It's already overgrown, man.'

'I do it every day sir,' the old man got stubborn.

'Okay, but......' Rishi got hesitated. 'Okay, I'm also coming with you, if you don't mind.'

'No, no, you can go, I will go to my home after finishing it.'

'It's okay! Do your plantation than talking to me. I think it's the last light before the dark.'

The old man nodded positively.

In a few minutes, they entered, and the old man set out the baby plants and came out briskly. The darkness had covered everywhere, and the chill swift waves were slapping everyone hard on their cheeks.

'It's time for tea,' Rishi thought. 'Do you drink tea?' He asked.

As soon as Rishi took the tea word, Vedant's eyes got flashed with the whole morning incident. 'Yes,' he said hesitated &

afraid, 'But you should enjoy. I have to go. My family is waiting for me.'

'You are coming with me,' Rishi declared, and put his bicycle on the roof of the car and tightened it.

'Rishi I can go,' Vedant got afraid with his pure generosity. 'I can go on my own.'

'You gave me ride on your bicycle, can't I give a ride to you? This is unfair.'

Vedant was extremely confused about absorbing so much kindness which he never expected for the whole life. It was looking like a bluff for him. Their emotions were matched; companies were good, but their standards weren't the same, but still the old man killed his thought to not make a kind man feel sad and sorry.

In a few seconds, they sat in the car. It was very warm inside, making the old man feel cozy & comfortable. Rishi ignited the car and slowly accelerated it. The old man was glad to find warm waves that were passing through his naked skin like a feather.

'So, why did you set out new plants?' Rishi asked, gripping over the steering wheel, concentrated and free of mind at the same time.

'I can't tell you the whole story, but I feel good when I grow plants on my own. It's like love for me. I feel they are the evidence of our lives; to be grown together and ended up alone and strong in the end. We all go to our ways. I love how trees stand alone and silent and don't even cry when they get hurt.'

'You are philosophically very right, I never thought I'm with a man who knows much about life & love.'

'Sir, I'm an ordinary man, keeping everything simple.'

'Simple is rare, my friend.'

They were talking like the truth was in the air, wanted to be revealed. After a few minutes, they crossed Betwa River Bridge where the waves were roaring, but everything was very quiet inside.

'Now, we will drink hot tea,' Rishi winked and parked his car near the same shop that the old man visited in the morning. Both came out of the car, but one was extremely worried.

'Two cups of tea,' Rishi ordered the tea seller.

'Okay sir!' the tea seller gestured respectfully, but got furious as he saw the same old man standing near him.

'You fool, you come here again,' the tea seller shouted.

Rishi got jumbled.

'Hey what did you say?' Rishi yelled his words before the old man could say anything.

'Sir, this man doesn't have money and comes to drink tea every day!' The tea seller explained.

'So, you think you can disrespect him for this?' Rishi shrieked. 'He's my friend and you will give him whatever he wants. Don't you dare to disrespect him ever. Okay?'

'But!'

'Am I clear?'

'Yes sir!'

'Here's some advance, and he handed over a few big notes to him. 'Don't forget, I can come again if I ever find out something fishy.'

'No, sir it's okay!'

'Good!'

The kullad tea was ready and, in a moment, they were holding cups from their curves.

'This feels so good,' Rishi's eyes got a super shine.

'What?' the old man asked carelessly.

'Holding cup from the sides, feeling warmth!'

Vedant nodded positively, but still finding bizarre by seeing his kindness towards him. He was entirely clueless, but anyway he took the first hot sip; the same that fell on the road in the morning. How the same day had despair and blissfulness for the same moment. He was proud but confused. They both were sipping hot tea, slowly, speaking nothing like both were thinking something deep & divergent. Finally, the tea got ended with the day. They both sat in the car and Rishi dropped him in front of his small home, which looked like an old toy, but he ignored and took his way to reach the hotel near Betwa River, the Betwa Retreat.

Both spent their day very well but the old man had no sleepiness and heaviness in his eyes & still thinking; kindness has some boundaries and Rishi had already crossed it. It was a rare time when the talkative man was silent & thinking, and he wasn't even astonished for the whole life before, even when people hurt him. For him, hurting was more acceptable than kindness. What a bizarre world we are living in.

Chapter 2

The next day came like every other day, but it was a little pole apart for the old man who had already anguished in his life. The clock was prompt, chasing the time of 7 o clock. That day, Vedant decided to bath in the Sacred Betwa River, followed by a hot tea. He still remembered that he could take tea from the tea seller and anything that he wanted.

'That's a good idea,' the old man murmured, thinking about a free tea and some breakfast, but suddenly wise brain cells teased him badly.

'I can't take it,' the old man ordered himself. 'It's not from my money; even if some stranger had paid money, I can't take it. Vedant, have some self-respect,' he convinced himself, and initiated walking on the road, towards Betwa River. That day, he wanted to walk, thinking profoundly, without doing anything in between, even without peddling. Thrashing his own thoughts, he reached down the Betwa River, just below and near the bridge, where many children and people were enjoying the chill waves and harsh sunrays on their bodies. In a moment of joy, Vedant forgot everything, found a slow wave and jumped into it. As his body touched the wave, he got the best electrifying shock. He went deep down and came on the surface, naturally like a cork. When you get into cold water, first, you only feel cold until you aren't wet, then after, you relish every wave of chill water. The old man was enjoying the waves like a child who was seeing river waves for the first time. Unknowingly, he was very delighted, may be because of the warm gesture by Rishi. How one person changes everything. We don't need a crowd but a one who cares for us, genuinely for the whole time. I bet, the world will be so beautiful that you will always want to live forever.

With that felicity inside his soul, he was patting waves, feeling the warm sun on his ageing body. Experiencing that constant happiness, suddenly his eyes got wet but already wet with water. No one knew he was crying there, unknowingly looking for someone to hug him firmly. The moment got gloomy, like only the clouds were bursting on his head. He was continuously wiping his tears with the wet hand but making it more wet. Everyone can leave you, but remember God is always listening; God is always listening to you. As he raised his head up, wiped his last tear, he saw Rishi first, far away, drinking tea on the other side of the bridge. As soon as he eye-contacted, Rishi also saw him, and waved his left hand positively to greet him. Orchha is really a small town & you can get passed by the same people many times, but sometimes people live in families, actually live too far away in a home. Distance doesn't matter. Love and efforts matter.

'Hey sir!' Rishi raised his voice high that everyone in the river heard him. At first, everyone saw both of them and then ignored in a blink. Vedant got less surprised like he was waiting for him silently. A shine of smile was wavering on his lips. He got happy like a child seeing his father for the first time. While controlling unknown emotions, the old man waved his hand, frequently, raised his eyebrows a couple of times and indicated him to come down towards the river.

Rishi nodded his head, threw kullad and made his way by slicing tiny stones under his feet, then jumping on the big stones, and reached near the old man with a smile, Hey man, don't you feel chill waves on your body?' Rishi asked while catching his breath. 'I'm still freezing here even with two pairs of woollen clothes.'

'Haha, absolutely not!' the old man laughed more happily, like it was forced. 'Come on sir, you are a young man. Come into the water. This is a natural stream; warm and pure. Once you are in it, you would forget the chill waves.'

'Oh, no, no,' Rishi refused, still frightening.

'It's okay, sir, I'm here. Nothing will happen,' the old man tried to convince him.

After a deep quick thought, Rishi agreed and nodded positively. He removed all his warm clothes and threw them on the stone near a slow stream. As he got in the underwear, a cool wave passed through, making him shiver. He sneezed while squeezing his hands, insanely, searching for warmth.

'Oh, I can't do that,' Rishi refused again. 'I can't do that.'

But this time, Vedant got agreed and felt right about not forcing him again, but Rishi felt like he was missing an opportunity to feel pure water on his temperate body. As the thought struck his mind, he came down slowly into the water, struggling with catching his breath. Slowly his body was adjusting and, in a few seconds, he got completely wet.

'Wohoooooo' he yelled in excitement, so high that he forgot he was in a public place. People ignored it because they all were experiencing the same thing.

'Thanks, young man,' Rishi appreciated the old man. 'All I can say, I have never experienced such energy throughout my body in years. This is incredible, man. This is incredible.'

The old man nodded positively with a smile. 'Enjoy sir, enjoy!'

They both were floating on the surface of the water, perceiving small waves coming from far, one after another. Every drop was fresh, untouched and loving.

A few minutes ago, the old man was wiping his tears and now in happiness state, but somewhere hiding something that needed to be revealed.

'Did you come here alone?' Vedant asked on purpose.

'Alone means?' Rishi counterquestioned casually, enjoying splashing.

'You came to Orchha alone?' The old man asked again with courage. 'How many members are in your family?'

The happiness ended like a moment ended too soon. Rishi's face got gloomy and pale. It was the first time the old man was seeing a deep silence on his face. In a second & jerk, Rishi came out and sat on one of the big stones near the stream, and the old man was still floating and fighting with the slow waves.

'There's no one in my family. I'm all alone, sometimes lonely,' Rishi announced, voice getting deep and sad. I ran away from my home when I was seven. A strange man raised me lovingly like his own son, but last year he passed away too,' he continued while a few drops of tears came out from his charming eyes.

The old man got shocked and emotional at the same time. He didn't know how to comfort a man who was crying because he was still struggling with his own tears.

'It's okay, sir,' Vedant said a few words to comfort him. 'Sometimes it happens. Life always plays like this.'

'Why did you run away?' The old man asked with curiosity & a little fear.

'It's a long story, sir,' He smiled and wiped his tears. 'By the way, I'm getting married next year.'

'I don't know what's happening in the hearts of your parents,' the old man got emotional.

'Do you want something to eat?' Rishi interrupted, ignored the old man's question.

The old man smelled the end of the argument and didn't ask again. 'No sir, it's okay. Now, I will directly go to my home.'

The deep talk got vaporised into thin air. Rishi started wearing clothes fast, ignoring the old man, like for purpose. Before the old man came out of the river, Rishi was ready to leave.

'I need to go,' Rishi announced, carelessly. 'You should also go to your home. Bye.'

'Okay sir,' the old man nodded, wanted to say something, but wasn't able to accumulate strength because who the hell he was for Rishi, just a stranger who talked too much and understood a little. He suppressed his own thoughts & convinced his mind for home.

Rishi left while the old man was still in the slow waves of the river. He had tears in his eyes, like hiding a big gloomy life behind it.

Sometimes we all want is loving too much to someone but suppress ourselves, so, we don't feel too much attachment & emotions. We try to walk away because we can't do anything

about it. Everything seems drowned in something that can't be explained in words.

A moment passed, Rishi got far away and vanished into the thin air while the old man was still silent, wanted to say something but to whom.

The day passed with shadowy & dead emotions. It was deep, slow and unanswered. The old man was in his room, gazing at the white ceiling that had nothing to say. It was a rare time when the talkative man was silent, thinking about a stranger who helped him for no reason. He was puzzled, and the room was making him more possessive with his silence and sadness. In a moment, he decided to go outside and get some fresh air, so he reached the front way of Orchha Fort. The fort was glimmering, vintage, gorgeous and classic like the king was still ready to give a strong message. As he got more interactive with the environment, his sadness got diffused and felt almost dead in his soul. A sudden smile came on his dried lips, and he stepped forward, crossing a bridge just before the entrance of the fort. On the both sides of bridge, there was a small canal, almost vaporised, left mold and green algae on the surface. The giant rocks were looking inky, and the bridge was on the height. It was always looking spectacular to see the far dried canal in the daytime. With mixed emotions, he was stepping forward but halted in between just before the entrance. A straight away thought came up that made him happy. He made his way to the opposite and took a pace to reach near the Betwa River Bridge. As he was having great energy reaching the destination, he got swift and finally reached there. The river was dark and angry. He looked on the right just before the bridge but got slow as he was also afraid of the destination.

Finally, he reached the Hotel Betwa Retreat. It's a vintage hotel of MP Tourism that can make you feel the chill waves & mesmerizing view of Betwa River from the hotel windows. First, he paused at the entrance while looking and understanding himself; but after that he accumulated an invisible strength and entered. It was dark but lit at the same time. Everything was perfectly placed, but in an urge to reach the reception, he ignored everything like killing happiness with his own sadness. There was an automatic door that opened as soon as someone stepped on the final stair. On the straight, he saw a reception where a girl was speaking on the landline, completely well dressed and mannered.

'Hello ma'am,' he made a good respected gesture.

'Hello sir! how can we help you?' the receptionist asked in sweet & calm voice.

'Actually, I'm looking for a person named Rishi, he said in hope. 'Is there any guest of such name staying here?'

'One-minute sir!' the receptionist paused and made a call. After a few minutes on the call, she replied, 'sorry sir, we can't reveal such information. If you have any of your client number, kindly call him now.'

The old man got discouraged, 'But ma'am, I don't have his number. I'm an old man. Rishi, the man helped me a lot. I just came here to say thanks to him and nothing else.'

The receptionist thought. 'Okay!' she replied instantly. 'What was the name you said?'

'Rishi.... his name is Rishi.'

'Okay!' as soon as he said, she replied, 'He already checked out an hour ago.'

'Checked out?' The old man was astonished. 'Okay and where had he gone?'

'Sir, how can we say this! Kindly respect our hotel policy.'

'Okay ma'am! Thank you!' The old man got slowed down that he never had in years. The legs were crawling to the exit, but he wanted to rush back and check every room of the hotel, but in a moment, he got his real consciousness. With dark sorrow, he came out of the hotel, standing in the middle of a road that was almost empty and strong. To get his full consciousness, he went straight to the shore of the Betwa River, where there were sturdy stairs; and on the opposite side, the garden where he once sat in deep sorrow. Everything was the same; the sorrow, the expectations except this time he was on the opposite side, looking for Rishi and wanted to ask, what really happened when he was a child; why did he run away? Thoughts came, but he waited endlessly and made himself drowned. The night got much darker than before, but in the end, his courage ended in silent pain. He stood up from dark stairs and took his way to reach home, where there was no partiality but love & warmth only.

Epilogue

Hope, what every human wants, to go ahead and overcome problems in life but sometimes hope is really an awful thing when you are entirely bone-weary, waiting for something good to happen, and it keeps longing, holding your throat till the end of your life. You just keep hoping for something that would never get to happen. Hope is really a terrible thing until we really do something on our own to make it a reality. Hope is ultimately the heroism of human initiation.

With the same perpetual hope, the next morning, Vedant took his way again to find Rishi. He was confident enough to find Rishi in a small place where he was already the talk of the town. Unlike talkative, he was completely different that day; silent and feeling like something was eating him gradually. Something was connected yet unconnected. To find him, he was standing near a road, in between the Raja Ram Temple and Orchha Fort, to get a glimpse of his red car somehow. He was very hopeful to find his car once. With his bicycle ready and fuelled his body with the tea and some snacks for which the amount was paid by Rishi, he was energetic to find him. From early morning to evening, the time passed slowest for him. He saw many red cars but didn't find Rishi in anyone. His hope got slowed down with time, wanted to run away and forget the thought, but still he was standing there for no reason. 'When God believed you a few times, why you don't believe in God,' he convinced himself, and continued. Somehow, he was hopefully true. Finally, a same red car just passed near him when he was only dreaming for him. The slowest eyes caught the moment very late, and the velvet car vanished to the other way.

'Oh my god,' the old man shouted inside, sat on the bicycle and started peddling with his entire energy. His adrenaline hormones were on peak and heart was almost pounding on his chest, but the speed of the car was much more than that. The car accelerated high and vanished. He got afraid, but still paddling in the darkest way. He was paddling like he got the way of his life. After an hour of exhausted paddling, he reached in between the silent woods where the car was on the left side, still untouched, indicators working, headlights on, and he could only experience the sound of the wind with some irritating noise of the insects.

His paddling got slowed down because it was the only loud noise that was piercing his ears. He left his bicycle in between, walked and reached near the door mirror and tapped on it a few times.

'Si...sir?' The old man stammered in panic and cold. The darkness was still higher than his expectations.

'Oh, sir?' Rishi exclaimed like he wasn't ready to see him. He was sitting inside in a pure white shirt whose first few buttons were opened and he had a lavish cigarette in his right hand, diffusing fumes into the whole car.

'Come inside!' He ordered.

As Vedant wanted to talk to him, he walked, opened the left door, and entered. He was smoking high but the odour wasn't that disturbing. In a moment, he ignored and asked, 'are you all right sir?'

'Yeah absolutely,' the old man declared without hesitation, inhaling fumes in style.

'Okay, okay sir,' Vedant calmed down. 'Sir, as you were going in tears, I thought I wanted to ask, why did you run away!'

'Haha, Right now?' Rishi got surprised & laughed 'I think I'm not ready to talk to you right now. You are a good person but...'

'But...sir,' Vedant got curious and afraid.

'I can't tell you because it's too close to my heart & life,' Rishi's voice got higher.

The old man nodded, opened the door and started walking towards his bicycle. Rishi was still silent, but in emotions, he broke out.

'Hey, young man,' Rishi called him, after pulling down the black mirror.

The old man looked back instantly, like he was waiting for that moment.

'Come and sit,' Rishi ordered him again.

He steered back the car straight and allowed him to sit.

'Can we go somewhere else to talk?' Rishi asked. 'What about your home?' He declared before the old man could say something.

The old man wanted to deny, but somehow his mouth got stitched in the expectation of his life's answer. His silence got converted into affirmation.

Without saying anything further, Rishi turned to the opposite side and accelerated the car into the thin cold air. In a few minutes, he parked a car in front of the old man's vintage home. During the journey, everything was damn silent like a big silence would get broken in a few minutes.

'So, you live here?' Rishi asked with a blank face.

'Yes sir', he nodded. 'You forgot, you had already come here when you dropped me here for the first time.

'Oh, I got it. I know I know.'

After a small talk, Rishi locked the car and they stepped up rapidly to reach the first floor. It was entirely dark and gloomy, like they had entered the woods, waiting for its moon. The room had a tumbledown door, completely destroyed, wanted to be vanished, but still standing to protect his house of only one room. Indeed, it was entirely a home of only one room that was protected by a weak door. In a second, Vedant unlocked it while Rishi was looking here and there, exploring and answering nothing.

They entered the room, first thing they noticed, it was a small cube-shaped room. It was entirely pitch dark except for some rays that were coming from the moon. As Vedant tried to turn on the light, the bulb didn't illuminate, may-be electricity had gone. There was nothing in the room except a weak cot in one corner, and a small rectangular window that was near the ceiling, too high like many prisons have.

'Can I sit here?' Rishi asked, still absorbing the room.

'Of course, sir,' Vedant stammered, finding and accepting himself as the poorest person in the world.

'Do you want something to eat?' The old man asked in fear, in the hope he would deny it because he had nothing to serve.

'Okay,' he replied in a positive gesture, but the old man got disturbed and afraid for long.

The old man nodded and went into a very small kitchen that was revealing nothing like a kitchen. It was neat and clean, and nothing else. In a minute, the old man came back with a small glass of hot water, which was vaporising slowly.

'Sir, I'm saying it truly, I have nothing to eat. I don't have anything to give it to you,' he declared in sorrow and handed over the glass of hot water to him.

'This hot water is good Young man,' Rishi smiled & comforted him. 'Why do you feel so poor of yourself? You are alive and healthy.'

'Money is everything,' Vedant declared without a thought. 'I'm sorry, sir, you have everything, that's why you're talking like this. Rich people always say, money is nothing; money doesn't matter. I don't have money and that's why I know the value of money. We humans value things once they are gone.'

Rishi nodded positively in respect. 'I think you are right sir,' he replied, sipping the glass of hot water. I still remember how my mother made me Maggie and a cup of milk coffee when I was a child. Those were the happy days. See, now I have become a successful man and still have nothing to share anything with anyone. We both have something missing in the pieces. Am I right?'

'Yes sir' the old man oscillated his head up and down.

'So, you asked. why did I run away from my home?' he smiled, revealing less happiness. The old man was still standing, listening to everything with a strange silence.

'My dad was a cruel man,' Rishi announced in pain. 'He was really a cruel man and he never came back for me in years even I'm still living my life alone. He never came back,' he repeated. 'He only ran towards success and now, what I'm doing, living my life for the sake of success only. What do you think, what am I doing into the woods? Living my life? Finding peace in deep rivers? No, I wanted to forget everything that's almost ended in my soul decades back.

The hot water ended and the old man was in a few tears. Rishi stood up and took a glass in the kitchen where a few sharp rays of the moon revealed a picture of a young lady on the wall. The black and white photo was well lit with the bright moon rays. Rishi's eyes got astonished, teary and bulged for the first time, and as soon as he got to say something, Vedant also witnessed the incident. Rishi's eyes got more flushed out with the heavy tears that were bringing a mountain of emotions into his heart. His heart melted after a long time. Being so strong, he never felt so mixed emotions in a moment.

'Who the hell are you?' Rishi's voice got sharp but filled with deep sadness. 'How do you know my mother?'

'Mother?' The old man's soul just came out of his body in a microsecond and settled. 'Your mother?'

The old man got to know everything and took a step toward him, but Rishi took his steps back, ended in the dark room.

'I didn't know you were my son,' Vedant's eyes got teary and his face got weary in seconds. 'I didn't know you were my son,' he repeated again.

'You aren't my father,' Rishi yelled, accepting his own pain. 'I never saw you for the whole life. I don't care for someone who doesn't look after his wife for the whole life. You are a piece of shit. You are a piece of shit.'

'I'm destroyed and I'm nothing now,' the old man elaborated. 'After you ran away, you never looked back on how your mother waited for you for the whole life, wanted nothing but you; but you ran away, left your mother in an endless pain. She's no more. She died of lung cancer when her last wish was to see you for the first & last time, but you vanished with your complaints. For the last 20 years I've been searching for you everywhere with the hope that someday I would talk to my son. I talked to everyone in town, city, states and everywhere where someday at last I would talk to my son and express my sorry to you. You would never believe how I talked to everyone, finding you in every young man's body.' Vedant continued with tears, hope and sadness.

'My mother died because of you because you never took care of her,' Rishi wiped his own tears. 'You were neither a good dad nor a good father. You were just on your business tours, earning money and never took care of your family needs. You deserve this. I hope you will rot in hell. You listen, you deserve this.'

Both were mourning with their complaints, reaching nowhere under the witness of the moon. The sadness was increasing in their room, and the arguments were increasing.

I still care for you, my son,' Vedant expressed slowly and tried a step toward hugging him, but Rishi pushed him back.

'I experienced you son when I was a stranger to you,' the old man said softly. 'You are a kind man. You help people for no reason and now you are pushing your dad away.'

'Because a stranger made me a man, but you didn't,' Rishi exclaimed. 'I can't hug you after perceiving so many broken elements from your character. There's nothing left. Emotions are dead and you are nothing to me,' he declared; the most bitter words of his life, took his way to the exit and slammed the door on his face.

Rishi left him without giving any hope. Everything had already ended before it began, but now it was excruciating for both to live life after that. It was like, after a long time, the strings of painful emotions got clashed and it was almost impossible to come out of it. While losing entire energy, the old man fell on the cold floor, carelessly, with no hope and happiness, just with a regret that would kill him slowly for the whole life. He laid himself on the floor for an hour, and that took all his body heat away. Suddenly, his eyes got opened & tried to see everything in the dark room. The electricity hadn't come yet, but he stood up with a blank face, trying to see the wall clock where 6:15 was partially visible. He opened the weak door and went out with an old bag in his hand.

There are a lot of desolate people wandering in the joyous crowd and he was one of them. He didn't bring the bicycle but wanted to walk, just walking even so much that he could reach the hell for doing such a thing for his family. Why he was even living, and for whom. His thoughts were troubling him too much. Before he was unhappy, but today he was sad & lonely; much lonely that he wanted to get drowned in it forever for the whole life. With such terrible thoughts, he reached the garden again that was opposite to the Sanctuary. He entered at such a pace that even the owner ignored him. He sat on the wet grass and started to dig out a place to bed out some tiny plants like he always did. Lost in his thoughts, he ended up digging three small holes and starting planting one by one into the deep and covering them slowly. He had big painful tears in his eyes, wanted watering new plants with his tears, but how much a person cries, it's not enough to make the whole tree grow. Society doesn't even care for the tears of a man who does everything for his family.

The garden man was staring at him like he was enraged at him. Every hell of a man was angry with that old man. With control of his tears, the old man tried to find the water bottle, forgetting he left it in the kitchen when Rishi asked for something to eat. The garden owner wasn't much encouraging to ask for a water bottle. Suddenly, Vedant saw a dark man who was coming towards him, slowly and speedily at the same time. It was all confusing for him knowing how far he had come, but, in a moment, he came close, passed him, and sat on the same bench that the old man usually used to sit on. He was nothing else but Rishi. The old man's eyes got shimmered with happiness.

'Tell me, why do you plant trees every day?' Rishi demanded an answer with a blank pale face. 'Tell me honestly.'

'You know,' the old man adjusted his voice to say more. 'We all are alone in our journey. Always meet new people but never make yourself lonely even with people. We all are alone like a tree moving with the wind; birds stay, people stay, sleep, live and finally leave but tree still stands like a strong creature. You can be crushed when you are planted. You can't be destroyed when you are strong.'

'So, you think you can make a few strong trees?' Rishi asked in a low cold voice.

'No, I just want to plant them; being strong is their own choice. Listen Rishi, when you talk, you seem happy but when you don't you seem like a silence to be spoken. You don't speak what you want. You speak what makes your heart happy. Your heart is sad somewhere, pouring happiness all over the world, seeking nothing but silence to be broken. You don't lie, my son;

you speak the truth what people want to hear. You try to break down strings of emotions so you convince yourself to not feel the pain of this world. You are a coward. You are a coward.'

Rishi was continuously listening to the words of his dad and seeing the slow waves of the river, but as he looked back, the big painful tears were already stained on his cold cheeks. His eyes were red and swollen, wanted to say something, maybe the truth. The old man got silent, but looking into his eyes. Both stood up in a rhythm; the sun rays were still appearing on their faces and somehow waiting for something. As soon as they stood up, they took slow steps and hugged each other tightly. The hug was so deep and intense that the tears were flowing from both sides. Suddenly, the sun rays vanished and the clouds came out of nowhere. It was so dark that it could make even the black colour dull. The three planted trees were waving like waiting for a rain, and the god listened, a few drops of rain fell down initially with a few drops and converted into big drops. The slow rain had converted into the heavy tears of God. Everything got wet including their eyes, that were being washed by the tears of God. Truly, God was with them, hugging them in the form of rain; otherwise who could expect and bore the cold showers in a 10-degree Celsius on a wintery day. Isn't it? After a minute, they got separated and the rain halted. The sky got clear, like having a feeling of sunrise at night. Nature is beautiful and strange. Sometimes the situations aren't right. No one is right or wrong because life goes like that; life really goes like that. Everyone has to die and who the hell wants to die with unsaid words, carrying deep emotions in their hearts.

When Rishi and Vedant got separated after a hug, first, the old man looked at the planted trees for a moment that were looking happy and moist but as he looked up to find Rishi, he vanished into thin air. No one was there except him, all alone, and the garden man who was still staring at him strangely for almost half an hour. His plants were wet, and except them, everything else was dry.

'Rishi,' he took his name in a high-pitched voice. 'Rishi! Rishi!' he continued until the garden man started him for a few seconds.

The old man ran towards the owner and asked, 'there was a man who was with me, where has he gone? I know you were staring us for a long time. You stare me every day. It's enough now. Where is he?'

'Who? What are you talking about, you, old man?' The garden owner asked in anger & confusion.

'The young man, my son who was with me. Come on, you saw him with me every day.'

'Are you mad? You fool. You never came with anyone. There was no one with you. You came here alone every time and that's why I was staring at you every day. You talk too much and now you are mad. Don't you remember, you told me, your son died at the age of seven and you came here to mourn on his death, and even that's why I always allowed you into this garden. I can't tolerate you anymore, you, old man,' the garden man got pissed.

'But my son was always here, everyone knows in the town,' he astonished slowly.

'You son is no more and no one knows you in this town. Only I know you. No one knows you. Are you understanding what I'm saying!'

'My son...My son,' the eyes of the old man got slow & heavy. 'My son was here. Everyone knows him.'

The garden man elaborated in a few words, 'You talk too much in your head. Do you think everyone lives in your head? Do you believe everyone is listening about what's going on in your damn brain?'

'But....my son...' the old man accepting the truth slowly, but all of a sudden, he ran away, leaving everything in the garden, including the memories and emotions he made. *His mind got silent, like it would never speak again, forever; an end to his emotions where no one would ever understand him, and eager to ask, why do you even talk to yourself when the whole world is talking to you? And why do you talk too much when the whole world isn't ready to listen to you?*

About the Author

Deepak Gupta is pre-eminently known for writing plain sailing, meticulous, and pragmatic Self-Help books. He's the author of **more than forty books** including **10 Principles to Beat Failure** that won **Google Best Choice 2018** & became **Top Seller on Google Play Store in 2019**. He has been garnering much acclaim for his **30 Minutes Read & 10 Principles Series**. Till now, he has received **800k+ readership** & **a lot of appreciation** from all over the world. He believes in writing & living best exceptional content from his subconscious mind. He loves to observe, absorb, and write on various social issues, inspirational truthful words, short stories, and heart whelming poetry. Also, he has travelled to many places in India like Manali, Rajasthan, Goa, Kolkata, Madhya Pradesh, Jammu, Dalhousie, and Mussoorie to bring originality in his work. He *releases new short books every month* to get readers to connect with the truth of life.

Deepak Gupta received his post-graduation degree from **Delhi School of Economics**. Also, when he's not writing, he can be found wandering on his **exquisite terrace garden**. He lives with his family in **Delhi, India**.

Keep in touch with Deepak via the web:
Instagram @authordeepakgupta
Facebook: facebook.com/authordeepakgupta
Twitter @authordeepakgup

Don't miss out!

Visit the website below and you can sign up to receive emails whenever Deepak Gupta publishes a new book. There's no charge and no obligation.

https://books2read.com/r/B-A-AQXE-ALQDC

BOOKS 2 READ

Connecting independent readers to independent writers.

Did you love *The Talkative Man: A Novella*? Then you should read *But She Didn't Come*[1] by Deepak Gupta!

Rashi, an intelligent and sensible girl in her mid-twenties, had been living in **North Goa since birth**. Being a real glass sucker and chain smoker, she was always one step ahead of teen life but shattering her adult life with over maturity and protectiveness. **Living near to those exotic beaches, she had no interest to gaze incessant sea, the kissing couples, and palm trees but when she met a near-perfect dazzling girl Nikita with a queer plan, her life got upended with the unanticipated affairs. As the tale moves ahead, new people make appearances with new**

1. https://books2read.com/u/md7ZBW

2. https://books2read.com/u/md7ZBW

expectations, stories, and demands.But She Didn't Come isn't the story of love but a poles apart anecdote of four shattered people who were lost in their own dreams of love & life.The Gist of GoaIf someone asks us where we should go to relish our life, we may suggest **Goa, the land of utmost freedom, and Bangkok, the cherry of Thailand**, but man, Goa has some high-spirited feel to get rolled into the vibes of the sea and to absorb it as an eternal party destination. We know people recognize Goa for pubs, bikini girls, and the perpetual exultation of beaches. You can reach Goa and you would never come back with a tedious mind. When people choose to sleep at their home, the honest-to-goodness parties start in the pubs and bars of Goa. **You may see people dancing, holding beer cans, looking divergent, and crossing every limit to find the amusement of life.** Humans are bizarre, they can dance everywhere, open or close sky, and nothing matters to them until they get what they want. Shack parties on empty beaches, bars flooded with couples, and some strange lured people looking for life, explore sea at every best place, and the shore of the sea. **Goa is an exceptional & glamorous tourist place to explore love, life, beaches, and monotonous shots of vodka, wine, cocktails, or maybe juices for some authoritarian people.BONUSLove happens in a moment and it develops severely every moment. Moment after moment, we want to escape, fight over it but never run away. With passing time, it becomes strong to possess our soul and never fade away in our hearts. How hard we try, we can't escape and whatever we tell people, the memories always come in front of our eyes. Love is the strongest memory of true hearts, and that's why it is rare but irresistible too.**

Read more at https://www.authordeepakgupta.com.

Also by Deepak Gupta

15 Minutes Read
Common Sense in the 21st Century

30 Minutes Read
How To Deal With Haters
One Second Rule: How to take Right Decisions quickly
without Thinking too Much
Hard Decisions Easy Life: Bandersnatch & The World of
Possibilities
Sell Your Talent: How to Convert Talent into Money along
with the Personality Development
Ideas & Origami
The Anti-Suicidal Self Help Book
The Therapy of Peace: Illustrated Edition
The Rules of Being Highly Productive
How to Think Everyday
Bedtime Thinker
The Rules of Being Highly Skillful
Blockchain Technology: The Future

Modern Classics
The Talkative Man: A Novella

Power
The Power of Universe
The Power of Nothing: They say and We do

Year of Short Stories
But She Didn't Come

Standalone
Inspiring Life
Zero Degree: An Icy Thriller
She: She Heals Everything
10 Principles To Beat Failure: Illustrated Enhanced Edition
Beta 2020
She's the Sunflower: Heart Healing Poetry and Prose
10 Principles To Love Yourself
How To Heal Yourself
She: She heals everything
Skyfall: Your Heart Will Fall Too
The Girl With No Dreams
The Pigeon With Broken Legs: Modern Classics Children
Story

Average Mind: The World is not the Wonder. It's the Wonder which makes your World

Being Busy Is Not Always Productive: Stop Wasting your Time at the Wrong Place

Happiness Without Cause: Why Happiness was easy in the 19th Century but not in the 21st Century

Alone Than Lonely: How to Live Life without Attachment & Enjoy your Company

The Lost Child

The Power Pack of Short Stories: Box Set of Crime, Thriller & Suspense Stories

Earth 2200

Amazon Kindle & Google Play ebooks Pricing System: Maximize Your ebooks Sales

5 Principles To Dig Out Success

◇◇◇◇: Udhaar

The Little Book of Wise Quotes

Deepak Gupta Collection: The Complete Self Help Book (2015-2020)

Revenge

Revolutionary Love: Friendship-Love-Revenge: A Novel

The Man Who Forgets

10 Principles to Live Peacefully

The Untold Life of My Sage Mother

Watch for more at https://www.authordeepakgupta.com.